Freddie goes swimming

Nicola Smee

· little hare ·

I'd like to be able to swim like my fish.
So would Bear.

Mum takes us to the
swimming pool.

Not the big pool, the little learner's pool.

I'm ready!

But Bear's not.
He doesn't want
to get wet.

Mum says I won't swallow the water if I keep my mouth closed ...

...but it goes up my nose as well!

"You'll soon learn, Freddie" says Mum.

So I practise ...

and practise.

Until at last ...